The Legend of Lightning & Thunder

Published by Inhabit Media Inc.
www.inhabitmedia.com

Inhabit Media Inc. (Iqaluit), P.O. Box 11125, Iqaluit, Nunavut, X0A 1H0
(Toronto), 146A Orchard View Blvd., Toronto, Ontario, M4R 1C3

Editors: Neil Christopher and Louise Flaherty
Art Director: Neil Christopher

We acknowledge the support of the Canada Council for the Arts for our
publishing program.

Printed and bound in Hong Kong
by Paramount Printing Co., May 2013 #135350

Library and Archives Canada Cataloguing in Publication

Ikuutaq Rumbolt, Paula, 1990-
    The legend of thunder and lightning / by Paula Ikuutaq
Rumbolt ; illustrated by Jo Rioux.

ISBN 978-1-927095-28-7

    I. Rioux, Jo-Anne II. Title.

PS8617.K89L45 2013   jC813'.6   C2013-902416-6

Canada Council   Conseil des Arts
for the Arts   du Canada

The Legend of LIGHTNING & THUNDER

Written by
Paula Ikuutaq Rumbolt

Illustrated by
Jo Rioux

For Nipituuq

FOREWORD

Many years ago, we began encouraging elders and respected storytellers to share their versions of traditional stories through our publishing initiative. This work started slowly, but with the help of many Nunavummiut we now have great books based on Inuit folktales, legends, and myths. This Inuit story initiative began because we noticed that Inuit children seemed to have more knowledge of southern stories and European folktales than they did of the Inuit traditional stories that are part of their heritage.

Over the past several years, a new group of emerging Inuit writers has surfaced. These writers are helping to retell traditional stories in new ways for the contemporary generation of children. Paula Ikuutaq Rumbolt is one of these new Inuit writers. We are very excited that she was willing to work with us and trusted us with her writing. We know you will enjoy her retelling of this traditional story as much as we did.

Neil Christopher
Louise Flaherty

In the past, Inuit were always finding reasons to celebrate. After the long winter, singing festivals were held in the spring to show the people's happiness at finally feeling warm weather. Inuit travelled from camp to camp to celebrate with each other. During these festivals, they ate, danced, and sang together. By foot or by dogsled, people travelled great distances to share their happiness and celebrate with one another.

This was a time before stealing existed. No one knew what it was, as it had never happened to anyone. People were welcomed into neighbouring camps warmly, and no one worried that there might be thieves among them.

At one of these singing festivals, a brother
and sister tried to join a camp's celebration.
They were orphans—without parents or
family—and they had travelled for a long
time to get to the camp. The children were
very hungry. They looked longingly at the
fresh caribou being shared. But when they
approached, they were told that there was
not enough food for them.

These children were very hungry, and they could not travel any farther without food, so they waited until everyone began dancing and singing. With the camp folk distracted, the two siblings grabbed some pieces of caribou and crept away from the group.

The brother and sister ate quickly and quietly, so that their thievery would not be noticed by the camp folk.

Once finished, the sister whispered to her brother, "I'm still hungry. Help me look for more food."

He always did what his sister told him to do. She was two years older than him, and he felt that what she did and said was right. He never questioned what she told him.

Several of the families visiting this camp had left their belongings outside as they enjoyed the festivities. So, the orphans searched through the visitors' packs, looking for food. The little brother carefully investigated a bag that held a woman's sewing supplies, but only found two caribou-bone needles and thread wound around an antler.

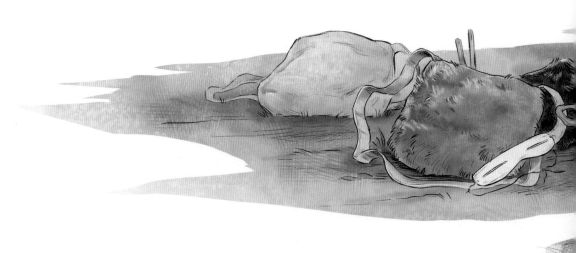

"No food in here, but do you want to sew something together with this needle and thread?" the little brother asked.

"No," his sister said, as she continued to search around the tents. "I am hungry."

They continued to look, but there was nothing to eat. Trying to ignore their aching stomachs, they searched for something to play with while everyone continued singing.

As the little girl searched, she found a dry, hairless caribou skin. She picked it up and knelt on the ground, waving the skin through the air and making sounds with it. She tried to make the skin sound like the waves on a windy summer night.

As the sister made wave noises, her brother found a piece of flint and a rock by a qulliq just outside the entrance to a large tent. He picked them up and shouted to his sister over the noise of the caribou skin and drumming, "I can practise making fires!"

She gave him a smile and yelled back to him, "Yes! This is fun."

After a while, the orphans decided that they should play away from the camp so they wouldn't be discovered by the camp folk, and off they went.

The brother picked up the rock. Holding the rock in one hand and the flint in the other, he brought them together. Small sparks shot out as he did so. When he saw the sparks, he laughed and continued to strike the two objects together.

Meanwhile, the sister was using the skin like a drum. Her knees were growing tired of kneeling, so she stood up and began waving the skin in the air and striking it with her hand. She shook the skin even faster and was exhilarated by the sounds it made.

She yelled out to her brother, over the booming sound of the skin, "It's amazing how many different noises you can make with one thing!"

"It is!" said the little brother, but he was more interested in watching the sparks fly when he struck the flint and rock together.

The two lost track of time as they played.

Suddenly, as he looked up and noticed the darkening sky, the little boy shouted to his sister, "They are probably finished dancing by now! What should we do?"

"We'll get into trouble. They'll scold us for stealing. We have to hide. They can't find out what we've done," she told her brother.

"So what should we do?" the boy asked his big sister.

"We need to hide where they will never find us," said the big sister.

"How about we turn into caribou?" the little brother suggested.

"No. They will hunt us, and then eat us. People are always hungry, and two caribou alone will be easy prey."

"How about wolves?"

"Still, they will catch us."

"Foxes?"

"No. They will try to catch us for our fur."

"Rabbits? Ptarmigans? Grizzly bears?"

"They will catch us!"

"Lemmings? Seals? Polar Bears?"

"No. No. No! They'll eat us if we turn into any animal," the big sister explained to her brother. "They will soon discover that we've stolen from them, but we can't turn into any animal because they will hunt us if we do."

The older sister, usually so quick to tell her brother what to do, did not know what she should tell him at that moment.

"What should we do, then?" the brother asked his sister, nervously.

"I have an idea. We will run away up into the sky," the sister told her brother. "They can't catch us there. We'll take the skin and flint with us."

"Are you sure? We'll never be able to come back to the ground."

"We will get into trouble if we stay, and we have no family anyway," the sister said, with sadness in her voice. "We have to hide in the sky."

So, the brother and sister ran away
into the sky. They brought with them
the items that they had stolen—flint,
rock, and dried caribou skin.

And now, when the children are bored or
feeling lonely, the orphan girl strikes the dry skin
with her fist, and the land trembles with the roar of
thunder. And, when the little orphan boy strikes the
flint together with the rock, the sky lights up with the
flash of lightning.

So, you see, because two orphaned children were neglected and ignored, we now have lightning and thunder in the world.

Contributors

ᐸᐅᓚ ᐃᑰᑕᖅ ᐅᒻᑉᐅᓪᑦ Rumbolt is from Baker Lake, Nunavut. She is currently attending Concordia University in Montreal. Growing up, formal education was strongly encouraged by her grandmother, alongside traditional Inuit beliefs. After high school, Paula attended Nunavut Sivuniksavut in Ottawa. There she learned much about Inuit history and culture. She realized how important it is to connect with her culture and began to learn as much as she could after her year in the program. She returned home for a year and learned how to sew, spoke to the elders in her community, and began to feel a very strong connection to her culture.

Jo Rioux was born and raised in Ottawa. An artist from an early age, she was eventually drawn to children's books, illustrating *Sword Quest* for HarperCollins and the graphic novel series A Sam and Friends Mystery for Kids Can Press. Her love for the comic medium spurred her to author her first graphic novel series, Cat's Cradle. She lives in the lush suburbs of her hometown, where, when not working at her drawing desk, she can be found nestled within a pile of books.

The Shadows that Rush Past
The Arctic is filled with folktales and legends about dangerous creatures and evil beings. Gifted Inuit writer Rachel A. Qitsualik introduces young readers to some of the most frightening creatures found in Inuit mythology in this collection of scary Inuit folktales.

The Orphan and the Polar Bear
In this unique Arctic folktale, shared by Inuit elder Sakiasi Qaunaq, a mistreated orphan is rescued by an unlikely friend and taught the skills needed to survive.

The Legend of the Fog
Throughout the Arctic, storytellers share stories of how our world came into being. This eerie retelling of the origin of fog from Cape Dorset elder Qaunaq Mikkigak will delight all children who have an interest in mythology.

Kaugjagjuk
Versions of the legend of Kaugjagjuk are shared by storytellers across the Arctic. The stories tell of a young boy and girl who become separated from their parents and eventually find themselves in a camp of unkind and selfish inhabitants. Inuit writer Marion Lewis lovingly retells this legend for modern audiences.

The Giant Bear
The fearsome nanurluk—a giant polar bear found in Inuit traditional stories—is brought to life by Taloyoak-area elder Jose Angutinngurniq. This folktale tells of a brave and quick-thinking hunter who encounters this powerful monster and must try to save himself and his family.

Arctic Giants
Stories of giants, some kindly and some terrifying, can be found throughout the Arctic. After spending over a decade interviewing Inuit elders and researching traditional stories, author Neil Christopher has assembled a complete collection of Arctic giant tales from around the North.

If you are interested in exploring the world of

Inuit myths and legends,

consider the following books:

Iqaluit • Toronto
www.inhabitmedia.com